DATE DUE

FEB 6 '84	MAY 17 1986	
MAR 31 '84		
	FEB 12 1987	
MAY 7 '84	MAR 14 1987	
MAY 28 '84	NOV 7 [illegible]	
JUL 5 '84	OCT 22 1988	
AUG 1 '84	MAR 31 1990	
AUG 25 '84	SEP 12 1992	
NOV 1 '84	OCT 31 2009	
JUL 18 '85		
SEP 5 '85		

ARNOLD OF THE DUCKS

ARNOLD OF THE DUCKS

by Mordicai Gerstein

Harper & Row, Publishers

Arnold of the Ducks

Printed in the United States of America. For information address Harper & Row, Publishers, Inc., 10 East 53rd Street, New York, N.Y. 10022. Published simultaneously in Canada by Fitzhenry & Whiteside Limited, Toronto.
First Edition

Library of Congress Cataloging in Publication Data
Gerstein, Mordicai.
Arnold of the Ducks.

Summary: Mistaken for a fish by a nearsighted pelican and deposited with a family of ducks, young Arnold learns to swim, fly, and eat like a duck until his curiosity finally leads him back to his human family.
[1. Ducks–Fiction 2. Babies–Fiction] I. Title.
PZ7.G325Ar 1983 [E] 82-47735
ISBN 0-06-022002-3
ISBN 0-06-022003-1 (lib. bdg.)

For Jesse and Aram

ARNOLD OF THE DUCKS

One hot May morning, while the sheep dog Waldo snoozed in the shade, little Arnold was scooped out of his wading pool by a near-sighted pelican and carried off.

His mother, who had run into the house to get him some apple juice, saw it happen from the kitchen window. She screamed, but it was too late.

The pelican gained altitude and headed for the sea.

It had happened so fast, all Arnold knew was that suddenly it was dark and smelled of fish.

He started to cry and kick and scream.

The startled pelican did a double roll and a flip.
Arnold tumbled out.

They were over the marshes, and Arnold landed in a nest of freshly hatched ducklings.

Mrs. Leda Duck, the mother, had gone off for a few minutes to find some snacks for her new family.

When she got back she was very surprised to find Arnold.

"Were you here before, or are you a late hatcher?" she asked him. "My goodness," she thought, "this is not a good-looking duckling!"

Arnold started to cry. "Mama!" he cried. "Mama, mama!" All the ducklings began to quack and cry also.

"Now, now," said Leda, and fed them all sweet marsh grass, and some baby mosquitoes. They liked that, and quacked for more. Arnold too.

"Welcome, all of you," said Leda. "Welcome to the wonderful world of ducks!"

Arnold was trained along with his duck brothers.

"First the duck walk," said Leda. "Pay attention, all of you. This is how it's done. Quackstep one,

and step quack two, and step one quack..."

"What kind of a duck is that?" Three house sparrows were giggling and pointing at Arnold. "Why, it looks more like a monkey than a duck," they laughed.

"And look!" chirped the littlest one. "It has no feathers!"

"Oh dear," said Leda. "Come children, let's give him some of our extra feathers, and dress him up a bit."

Using mud and marsh slime, they stuck feathers all over Arnold's body. The sparrows thought it was a joke, but they helped too.

When they were finished, Arnold did look a little more ducklike.

Eventually, he learned to do an acceptable duck walk—though he was better at hopping, which his duck brothers couldn't do at all.

Next, Leda led them right into the marsh.

"Swimming lessons, children," she said. "Quack and paddle, quack and paddle..."

Arnold went right in, and went right under.

He swallowed some marsh water the wrong way, he coughed and splashed, but finally he did an acceptable paddle.

It was a dog paddle, but Leda chose to ignore that. She knew he would never be your average duckling, but he tried hard and he was very lovable. In fact, she might have loved him a little more than the others, though she'd never have admitted it.

The surprising thing was how easily Arnold took to flying. Taking off from water is not easy. Even for a duck.

Arnold began by kind of hopping along through the shallows and waving his arms. The hops became leaps with a lot of flapping.

Then he flew, and he flew well.

He liked to rest on the breeze till he saw a fish. Then he'd dive.

Unlike most ducks, Arnold liked to land in trees. It made Leda very nervous.

"Come down from there, dear," she would plead. "You might fall."

The sun rose and set, and the seasons passed quickly. Arnold grew much bigger than his brothers. They kept having to refeather him.

From time to time a story would appear in the news about someone having seen a huge duck with a short bill. Most people thought it was just another UFO.

In fall Arnold and his family would fly to Florida to spend the winter. Leda carefully avoided people, and taught her ducklings to avoid them too.

In Florida Leda had some relatives that were flamingos. They would paddle around the swamps fishing and quacking.

One spring, just as they were nearing their home marsh after a long flight, Arnold saw a large, shiny, red-and-silver thing fluttering in front of them.

"What is it?" he asked Leda.

"It's just a kite," she answered, "and it's a people thing, so for goodness' sake, stay away from it!"

But Arnold couldn't stay away from it. Leda didn't see him turn and fly back.

The kite was covered with stars and stripes, and it seemed to dance with him.

As he flew round and around it, he began to remember things. Things from another life.

Suddenly the wind changed, and the kite lurched at him. The string wrapped around his arms and legs.

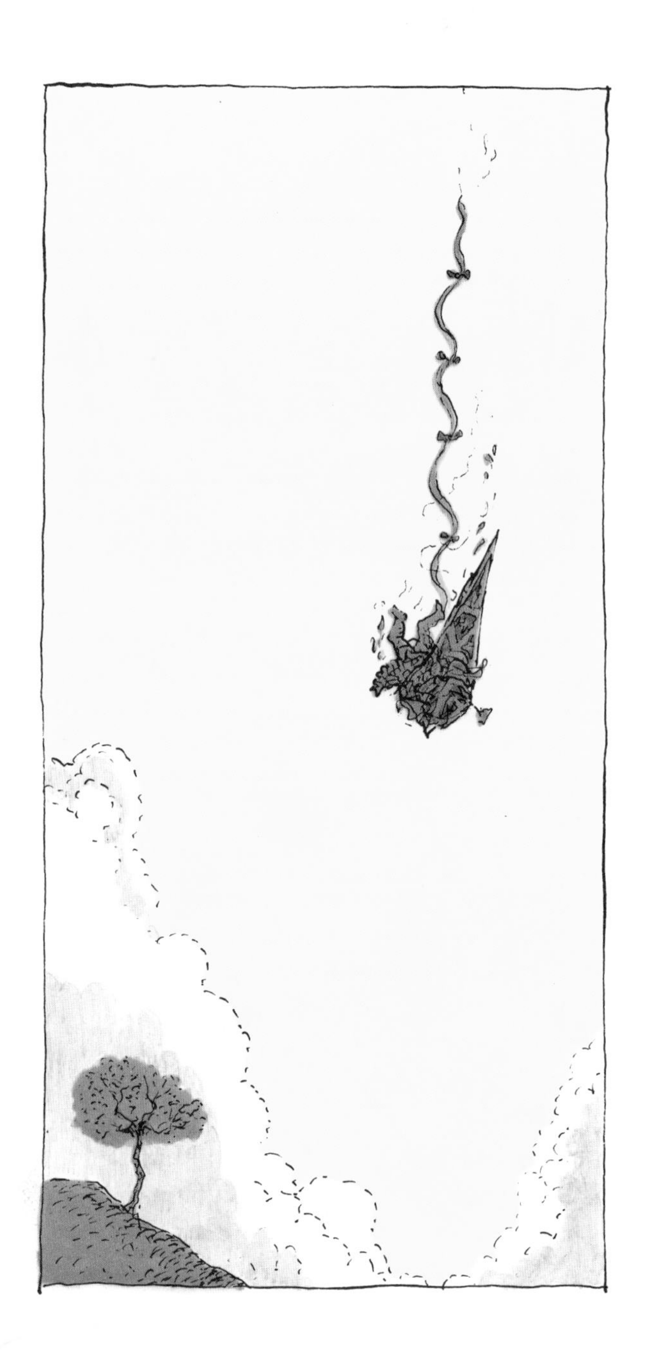

He struggled, but the kite went into a dive. He plunged to earth.

Arnold was shaken by his fall, and he'd hurt his shoulder. When he looked up, a huge shaggy sheep dog was standing over him.

He and the sheep dog looked at each other. Then the big dog sniffed him all over, which made Arnold giggle. He was ticklish.

Then the dog sneezed and very gently picked Arnold up in his huge mouth.

He carried him out of the park and through the streets.

"Where are you taking me?" quacked Arnold. The dog didn't answer. Partly because he didn't understand, and also because his mouth was full of Arnold.

Finally he went up the walk of a little white house and scratched at the screen door.

A woman came to the door. It was Arnold's real mother. "My goodness," she said. "What have you brought us today, Waldo?"

Arnold didn't recognize her.

She looked more closely. Arnold was covered with feathers and mud and wrapped up in the remains of the kite.

She didn't recognize him either.

"Whatever it is, it needs a bath," she said.

She and Arnold's father, her husband, put the duck child into a nice hot bubblebath.

All the feathers and mud and marsh slime washed away.

"It's Arnold!" screamed his mother, and she fell into the bathtub.

Arnold flew out and flapped around the house, but without his feathers, and all wet, he didn't fly too well.

His father finally caught him in the dining room.

His mother and father both cried and hugged him and kissed him. They had looked everywhere for him.

It took several weeks to retrain Arnold from a duck to a human child.

They patiently taught him how to eat with his "wings," or hands, and not his "bill." Later came spoons and forks and knives.

They taught him to speak English, and a few words of Spanish and Yiddish. He told them all about his life as a duck. They were amazed.

At night, tucked into his bed, sometimes he dreamed of his duck mother, Leda, and his duck brothers.

The years passed, and one fall day, as Arnold was on his way to school, he heard a familiar sound. He looked up and saw a family of ducks flying south.

"Mother!! Brothers!! Wait!! It's me!" he shouted. "It's me!"

Leda turned her head, startled. Was it the voice of her long-lost duckling? She looked down, but all she could see was a boy, waving his arms and shouting.

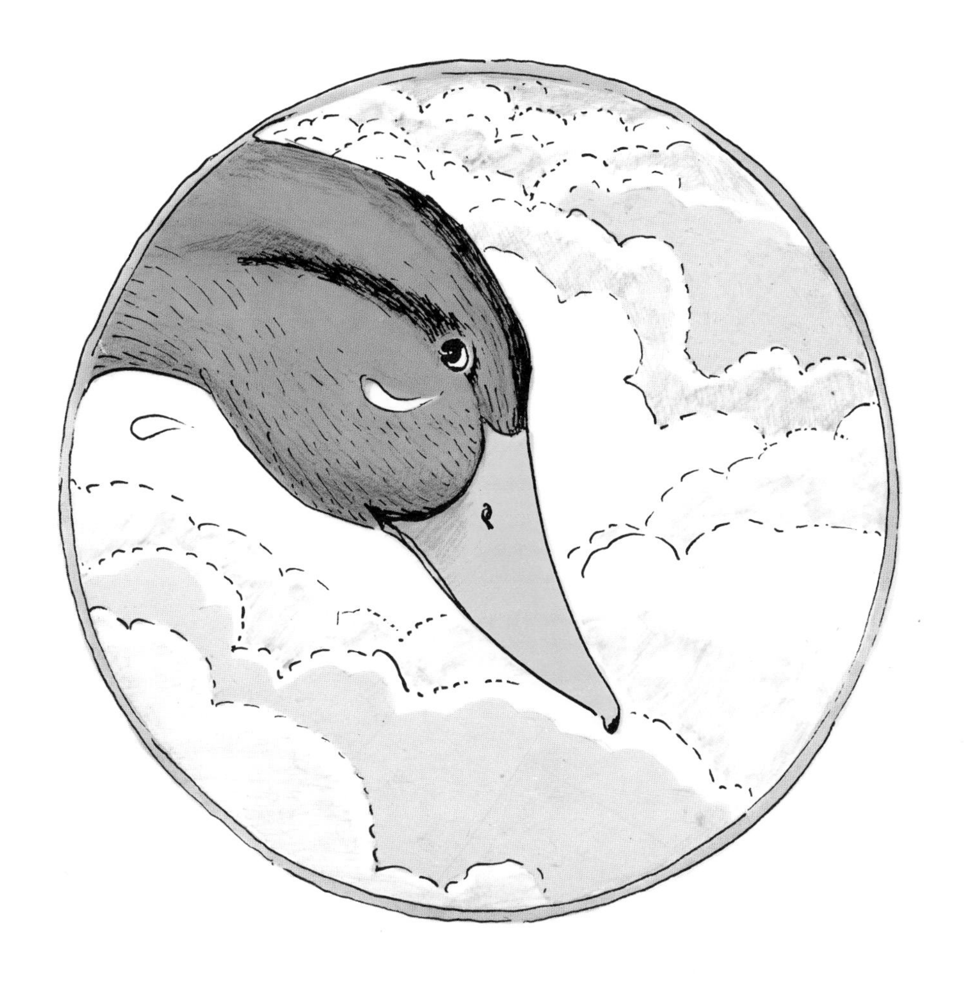

"Just my imagination," she thought, as a tear blew from her eye.

Arnold started to run after them. He had kicked his shoes off, and thrown down his books and jacket, when he stopped.

He wasn't a duck. He was a boy.

He watched his old friends till they disappeared into the clouds.

Then he picked up his things and went on to school.